All summer long, the woods had been warm and
green. Flowers had bloomed and faded. Now in their
place grew tasty nuts and fruits. To the animals born
that year everything was new: buttercups and

# The MAGIC TREE in WINTER

## By Hannah E. Glease

## Illustrated by Gillian Embleton

**Piccolo Picture Books** Pan Books · London and Sydney

In deepest woodland stood an oak
That often smiled but never spoke

Upon its trunk so old and lined
It had a face for *you* to find

For no grown-up can ever see
The features of a magic tree

The animals and birds all knew
Exactly where this wise tree grew

They gathered in the leafy glade
And took protection from its shade

Two squirrels in its mouth had found
A safe dry home, well off the ground

And just above, beneath its brow
An owl perched on a bending bough

Some badgers burrowed underground
In tunnels spreading far around

And butterflies and birds and bees
Flew in from all the other trees

This story tells of an owl's pretence
And the joke we had at his expense

butterflies, blackberries and bright new cherries, mushrooms and bumblebees, and acorns from the magic tree. When autumn came, cold winds blew. The animals shivered as they watched the leaves fall.

The little ones tried in vain to stick the crinkly
brown leaves back on the bare branches of the magic
oak. "Oh, what can we do?" they asked the owl.
"We are warm with our fur. You are warm with your

feathers. But the poor old tree is bare and cold."
The owl and the oak tree laughed in silence. For
the magic tree had enjoyed its leafless rest for
more winters than they could ever guess.

Then, even worse, the stream froze over. "What will happen to the frogs and the fish?" asked the badgers. "Let's look and see," quacked the ducks. And what do *you* think they saw in the water?

"That's odd," they each said to the magic tree.
"No fish or frogs, all I saw was me." So the tree
sent the owl to tell them the truth, that the frogs
and the fish were alive and well.

"The frogs are asleep in their burrows," hooted
the owl, " and the fish are still swimming under
the ice. It's not my fault you can't see them."
The animals looked again but still could not see.

"Show us, please," they asked the owl. But even
he could not see beneath the ice. So he pretended
not to hear and flew off as fast as he could. *You*
can see the hidden creatures, can't you?

One night the animals awoke to a strange snow-
covered world, all white. "Are there more trees
here than usual?" whispered the badger. "We're
sure there are," said the squirrels. "Oh, really,"

scoffed the owl. "Haven't you ever seen deer before? Their antlers look like branches." But in the darkness the animals still could not tell which were trees and which were deer. *You* can, can't you?

13

When the sun came up, the animals could easily see which were trees and which were deer. How they laughed at the first sight they saw. "Look at the owl," shrieked the squirrel. "He's asleep on an

antler instead of a branch," snorted the badger.
The owl woke up and, red in the face, flew back to
the magic tree – who had known all along that owls
are no wiser than you or me.

15

# Play and Learn

1  Help the children to tell you the story in their own words. Stop reading from time to time to allow them to tell you what happens next.

2  Ask them to show you the face on the magic tree and see if they can name the animals in the pictures.

3  Talk about the weather and how it changes through the seasons.

4  Explain that some trees shed their leaves in winter, like the magic tree, but others, such as pine trees, keep their leaves all year round. When you go out for a walk, get the children to collect these different types of leaves and compare them. Choose one tree and collect a leaf from it each month to see how they change colour and shape.

5  Play counting games. Ask "How many fishes are there on page 10? How many animals on pages 6 & 7?"

6  Explain how water turns to ice when it is very cold. Let the children watch an ice cube melt.

7  If it snows, go out for a walk and see if you can find footprints of animals and birds in the snow.

8  Ask: "Which is the biggest animal in the story? Which is the smallest?"

9  Find out which animal the children like best and help them to make up a story about it.